The Not So SCARY Story

The people of Hugsville were excited. Someone new was moving to the neighbourhood.

They didn't know who they were or what they were like,
but they were looking forward to meeting them.

Everyone gathered excitedly and watched as their new neighbour arrived in his moving van. They waved and said hello, but the new neighbour didn't say anything to them or wave back.

Instead, he rushed into his home and closed the door.

The neighbours were eager
to make a new friend.

But the new neighbour NEVER left
his home until the sun had set, which
seemed REALLY spooky!

He NEVER said, **"Hello"** or **"Good Evening."**

In fact, he always ran away when he saw anyone.

Sometimes all they saw was his long cloak.

It SWOOSHED,
SWISHED, AND SWEPT
everywhere he went.

Oscar was CURIOUS about his new neighbour.

A long cloak and only going out at night...

Could the new neighbour be a VAMPIRE?
Oscar NEEDED to know!

So one night, Oscar
decided to find out.

Oscar quietly followed as the long cloak

SWOOSHED, SWISHED,

AND SWEPT

through the city's streets.

But Oscar didn't realise that he
had been spotted.

With a SCREECHING squeak,
the new neighbour opened the park gates
and slipped through.

Oscar was getting nervous.
He had never been to the
park this late, and it
seemed like a much
creepier place with a
vampire around.

Walking past the swings and the murky
pond, Oscar scanned the park for his neighbour.

But he was nowhere to be found. And now
Oscar was in the park all alone...

Then Oscar spotted something
behind the tall oak tree.
As he picked it up, a shadow
jumped out and Oscar let out
a huge YELP!

His new neighbour jumped with fright and a tattered, little teddy bear flew from under the cloak and landed between them.

Oscar had never imagined that a vampire would own a teddy bear.

Carefully, Oscar picked the
teddy bear up off the
ground and handed it back
to his new neighbour, who
burst into deep sobs.

"What are you doing?
Why have you been
following me?"
he cried.

"Oh dear, I'm so sorry," said Oscar, ashamed.
"I got carried away. I thought you were a vampire!"

"I'm not a vampire. I'm Benjamin. I just like wearing my long cloak. It makes me feel safe. Meeting new people makes me nervous, so I like to hide behind my cloak and I explore the city at night when the streets are empty," wept Benjamin.

"It's so hard to make friends
when you're a bit different."

"This city is a big place," Oscar replied.
"There's a friend here for everyone.
We just need to get to know you.
I actually think your cloak is great!"

Benjamin's sad face
broke into a smile.

"I like wearing my soft winter
scarf even when it's not cold
outside. It makes me feel safe
too!" said Oscar.

He comforted Benjamin
and they walked
home together.

The next morning, Benjamin and
Oscar shared a hot chocolate

"I suppose we are all a bit
different," said Benjamin.

"But we can still be really good
friends," added Oscar.

And they both smiled.

P.S. - You should always try to be kind, polite, and welcoming to others,
just as Oscar learned to be. But not everyone will be as kind and polite as you,
so make sure you ask an adult before talking to someone you don't know.